Leaves to My Knees

By
Ellen Mayer

Illustrated by
Nicole Tadgell

STAR BRIGHT BOOKS
Cambridge Massachusetts

Published in the United States by Star Bright Books, Inc.
The name Star Bright Books and the Star Bright Books logo
are registered trademarks of Star Bright Books, Inc.

Please visit: www.starbrightbooks.com. For orders,
email: orders@starbrightbooks.com or call: (617) 354-1300.

Hardcover ISBN: 978-1-59572-959-0
Paperback ISBN: 978-1-59572-960-6
Star Bright Books / MA / 00110220
Printed in China / WKT / 10 9 8 7 6 5 4 3 2 1

Printed on paper from sustainable forests.

The author would like to acknowledge an early draft of
this book was supported in part by TERC under a grant
from the Heising-Simons Foundation.

Library of Congress Cataloging-in-Publication Data

Names: Mayer, Ellen, author. | Tadgell, Nicole, 1969- illustrator.
Title: Leaves to my knees / by Ellen Mayer ; illustrated by Nicole Tadgell.

Description: [Cambridge, MA] : Star Bright Books, [2022] | Summary: Camille
   is determined to rake her own knee-high pile of leaves. Includes note to
   parents and caregivers.
Identifiers: LCCN 2022013636 | ISBN 9781595729590 (hardcover) | ISBN
   9781595729606 (paperback) | ISBN 9781595729613 (paperback)
Subjects: CYAC: Leaves--Fiction. | Size--Fiction. | Measurement--Fiction. |
   African Americans--Fiction. | LCGFT: Picture books.
Classification: LCC PZ7.1.M385 Le 2022 | DDC [E]--dc23
LC record available at https://lccn.loc.gov/2022013636

For Elise and Jamie, my leaf
raker and leaf collector —EM

For Anthony; may you always
be a child at heart —NT

I've got my big jacket on.
Daddy helps Jayden with his little jacket that used to be mine.
Daddy says there's a surprise.

My own big rake!
It's perfect for raking leaves.
"Can you rake your own big pile of leaves?" Daddy asks.
"I can! I'll rake leaves all the way up to my knees!" I tell Daddy.
"Go for it, Camille!" Daddy says.

Jayden drags his little rake.
I carry my big new rake up on my shoulder.
Because I am serious—I mean business!

The leaves go **swush** when Daddy rakes.
They go **swish** when I rake.
They go **sweeeee** when Jayden tries to rake.

So many acorns and twigs!
My rake doesn't work.
It's no good.
"DADDY, HELP PLEASE!"

How will I ever rake leaves to my knees?
I sit down with my rake.
Daddy yanks out the twigs.
"You're good to go now, Camille," he says.

I step into my pile.
My pile is only up to my ankles.
Good for squirrels to jump in, that's all.

Jayden's pile is way smaller than mine.
It's not really even a pile.

"NO STEALING—FREEZE!"
I hold out my rake to guard my pile.
"Daddy's got more than me," I tell Jayden.
How will I ever rake leaves to my knees?

My pile is only up to my boots.
Good for kicking, that's all.
Back to work!

I rake bunches of leaves.
Daddy rakes bunches and bunches.
Jayden just collects leaves.

Wait.
"Oh no!"

"A BIG BREEZE!"
Lots and lots of leaves **whoosh** away.
Daddy and I just watch.
I will never rake leaves to my knees!

My pile is back down to my ankles.
Daddy and I sigh big sighs.
"Let's get going again, Camille," he says.

I throw off my jacket.
I grip my rake tightly.
I rake back all the leaves that **whooshed** away.
And some new ones.
I'm a raking machine!

I'm so tired.
I can't rake anymore.
I wonder—Do I have leaves . . .
All the way to . . .
My knees . . . ?

"Time for measuring!" says Daddy.
I hand my rake to Daddy.
I take a deep breath.
I step into my pile.

"TA-DA!"
"Way to go, Camille!" shouts Daddy.
 My pile is the perfect size for jumping.

"Move away," I tell Daddy and Jayden.
"This will be—BIG!"
I back way up.
"GO!" yells Daddy.
"GO!" Jayden yells too.

I run and leap the largest leap ever!
"WHEEEEEEEE!"

Jayden jumps in too!
We take a rest.
Then Daddy gives me a . . .

Really big squeeze.
Because I raked leaves all the way up to my knees!

A Note to Parents and Caregivers

In *Leaves to My Knees*, Camille uses the math of measurement as she tries to rake a knee-high pile of leaves. She measures by comparing her growing leaf pile to the height of her ankles, her boots, and her knees, and she describes sizes around her, using words like "big," "smaller," and "largest."

You can help children explore measurement, too. As you read this book, point out varied sizes in the illustrations, for example, "Camille's rake is much bigger than Jayden's rake." Or, "The pile goes up to Camille's knees. I wonder how high it would reach on Jayden."

As you go about the day with children, invite them to compare sizes of things around them. For instance, when sorting laundry together, ask, "How is my sock like yours? How is it different?" As children compare and contrast, they will notice and talk about sizes. They will also learn that measurement is part of everyday life.

—Marlene Kliman, Senior Scientist at TERC (Cambridge, Massachusetts)